Megalosaurus

Stegosaurus

Baryony...

Sty...acosaurus

Tyrannosaurus rex

For Caroline

First published 2016 by Nosy Crow Ltd
The Crow's Nest, 10a Lant Street
London SE1 1QR
www.nosycrow.com

ISBN 978 0 85763 583 9 (HB)
ISBN 978 0 85763 584 6 (PB)

Nosy Crow and associated logos are trademarks
and/or registered trademarks of Nosy Crow Ltd.

Text and illustrations copyright © Penny Dale 2016

The right of Penny Dale to be identified as the author
and illustrator of this work has been asserted.

A CIP catalogue record for this book is available from the British Library.

Printed in Turkey

1 3 5 7 9 8 6 4 2

DINOSAUR PIRATES!

Penny Dale

Pirate Dinosaurs speeding,
speeding across the sea.
Across the sea,
in their sailing ship.

Creak!

Captain dinosaur planning, planning the secret journey.

Busy dinosaurs working,
working hard on the deck.

Sleepy dinosaurs swinging,
swinging in
their hammocks.

In their hammocks,
till morning comes.

Snore! Snore!

Snore!

Excited dinosaurs rowing, rowing to the island. The island on the secret map.

Hot dinosaurs **digging,**
digging all day long.
All day long, **until** they find . . .
the **treasure chest!**

Heave ho!

Heave ho!

Heave ho!

Surprised dinosaurs roaring, roaring at the robber raptors.

Angry dinosaurs battling,
battling to save their ship.

Defeated raptors jumping,
jumping into the water.
Into the water and
swimming away.

Splash!

Splash!

Splash!

Victorious dinosaurs opening, opening their treasure chest.

Happy
dinosaurs
dancing,

dancing
and singing songs.
Pirate songs, all night long!

Yo, ho, ho! Yo, ho, ho!
Yo, ho, ho!

Jolly Roger

Pieces of eight

Lantern

Telescope

Pen and ink